Shout, Show and Tell!

Written by

Kate Agnew

Illustrated by

Lydia Monks

Green Bananas

First published in Great Britain 2004
by Egmont UK Ltd
239 Kensington High Street, London W8 6SA
Text copyright © Kate Agnew 2004
Illustrations copyright © Lydia Monks 2004
The author and illustrator have asserted their moral rights.
ISBN 978 1 4052 0875 8
10 9 8 7 6 5 4
A CIP catalogue record for this title is available from the British Library.
Printed in Singapore.

Daisy

Sean

Lily

For Alice and her friends at
Bounds Green School
K.A.

Daisy

On Monday Mrs Green asked the class to talk about their weekends.

Daisy put up her hand. But Mrs Green

chose Sean and Amber and Jack.

Daisy bit into her apple with a very loud crunch. Her tooth felt rather odd.

On Tuesday it was P.E. Daisy didn't
want to jump up high in case her
tooth wobbled even more.

On Wednesday Lee pointed to
the letters while they sang the
alphabet song.

Daisy sang very quietly because
of her tooth.

On Thursday Daisy really wanted

to wash up the paint-brushes.

Mrs Green said it was Joe's turn.

On Friday Mrs Green's class had

show and tell while they ate their fruit.

13

Daisy had forgotten to bring
anything from home. She felt cross
and fed up.

Mrs Green gave her an apple.

'Here,' she said, 'have a bite.'

Daisy had a bite. Her tooth wibbled

and wobbled and wibbled some more.

Then it came out, right in the middle

of show and tell.

Daisy put up her hand.

'Please, Mrs Green,' she said. 'I've got something I'd like to show.'

And Mrs Green chose Daisy first of all.

Sean

Jack and Daniel were playing in the jungle. Sean ran in with his dinosaurs. They made a big roaring noise.

'Sean,' said Mrs Green. 'Please play quietly.'

Sean went to see Amber and Dotun in the home corner. He woke the baby and the dressing-up clothes got a bit messy.

'Sean,' said Mrs Green. 'Please

play nicely.'

23

Emma was making bubbles in the
water tank. Sean thought a volcano
would be much more fun. He put
some red paint in the bottle.

WHOOSH!

'Sean,' said Mrs Green. 'You will have to stay in at playtime to tidy up.'

Sean put the paints in the corner of the cupboard.

Mrs Green came to see.

'Well done,' she said. 'You can go out to play now.'

But the cupboard door was stuck.

Sean was stuck inside. Mrs Green

was stuck too.

Oh, dear!

'Sean,' said Mrs Green. 'I think you
had better try shouting.'

Sean took a deep breath.

He pretended to be a lion and

roared as loud as he could.

HELP!!

Miss Wood came and opened the
door with a screwdriver.

'Oh my goodness,' she said.

'Were you scared?'

'No,' said Mrs Green. 'Not with

Sean here to shout for help.'

Lily

Mrs Green's class were making books.
They had to draw their homes and
the people who lived there.

Daisy drew her mum and dad and her brother and her new baby sister.

Dotun drew his mum and dad and
his brothers. Then he drew his auntie
and cousins, who sometimes came to
stay with him.

Jack drew his mum and his dad and his cat and his dog and his fish and his child-minder.

Lily drew her mum and their flat

with a big bowl of flowers. She felt

a bit sad.

'Oh dear, Lily,' said Mrs Green.

'You haven't got very far, have you?'

Lily started to cry.

Mrs Green had a think. She gave

Lily a hug and a new piece of paper.

Then she whispered in Lily's ear.

At playtime Lily was still busy drawing and cutting. But when showing time came she was ready.

I've finished!

Lily opened her book very carefully.

Now everybody could see all her houses

and all the people who lived there.

Dad's house had a new bed. Granny's
house had a swing in the garden.
Auntie Mary's flat was a bit messy,
but Mum still had her flowers.

And Lily was in all the pictures.